Beverly Cleary

THE REAL HOLE

Illustrated by DyAnne DiSalvo-Ryan

A Young Yearling Special

Published by
Dell Publishing Co., Inc.
1 Dag Hammarskjold Plaza
New York, New York 10017

Yearling ® TM 913705, Dell Publishing Co., Inc.

ISBN: 0-440-47521-X

Reprinted by arrangement with William Morrow and Company, Inc.

Printed in the United States of America

November 1987

2 4 6 8 10 9 7 5 3 1

D

Jimmy and Janet are twins. This means they have the same mother, the same father, and the same birthday, too. Jimmy always has Janet to play with, and Janet always has Jimmy to play with. Even though Jimmy and Janet are both four years old, they do not always like the same things.

Janet likes pretend things. She likes to pretend that a block is a cup of tea or that two paper bags are a pair of boots.

But Jimmy—Jimmy likes real things. He doesn't want to play with a toy hammer and toy nails. He wants to play with a real grown-up hammer and real grown-up nails. When Jimmy's father brings him a present, the first thing Jimmy asks is, "Is it real?"

One morning Jimmy said to his father, "I want to dig a hole. I want to dig the biggest hole in the world."

"That's a good idea," said Jimmy's father, and he found a place in the corner of the backyard where Jimmy could dig a hole.

Jimmy took his toy shovel and began to dig. He put the shovel into the dirt and pushed it down with his foot, the way he had seen his father dig. When he tried to lift the dirt—*snap, crack*—the handle of his shovel broke.

"Daddy! My shovel broke," cried Jimmy. "I need a real shovel."

"The real shovel is too big," said Jimmy's father, "but you can try." He brought Jimmy the real shovel, which was much bigger than Jimmy. Jimmy worked and worked, but the real shovel was too big and heavy for him. The hole Jimmy was digging was hardly a hole at all.

"I have an idea," said Jimmy's father. He went into the garage and came out with a shovel that was just Jimmy's size. "I had forgotten we had this," he said.

"Is it real?" asked Jimmy.

"Yes, it's real," answered Jimmy's father. "This is the kind of shovel soldiers use to dig trenches. It is called a trench digger."

"Real soldiers?" asked Jimmy.

"Real soldiers," answered his father.

While Janet played in her swing, Jimmy began to dig. The real shovel that real soldiers used was just the right size for Jimmy. He could never break the handle of this shovel. No, sir!

He pushed the shovel into the ground, lifted out
the dirt, and tossed it out of the hole. Push, lift,
toss. This was the way Jimmy wanted to dig.

When the milkman brought the milk,
he said to Jimmy, "Say, that's a real shovel
you have there! And that's a mighty big
hole you're digging!"

"I'm digging the biggest hole in the world,"
answered Jimmy, and he went on digging.

"My, what a big hole," said Jimmy's
mother, when she came outside to
tell Jimmy and Janet that lunch was
ready. Then she brushed the dirt off
Jimmy's jeans and emptied the dirt
out of Jimmy's shoes.

After lunch, while Janet galloped around on her
hobbyhorse, Jimmy went right on digging. Push,
lift, toss. The hole was almost up to his knees
when his mother came outside, brushed the dirt off
his jeans, emptied the dirt out of his shoes, and
took him inside for his nap.

Jimmy was so tired from digging all morning that he took a good long nap. When he woke up he climbed out of his bed in a hurry, so he could go outside and dig in his hole some more.

But when Jimmy opened the back door, he
discovered that Janet was already awake. She was
not only awake, she was out in the backyard sitting
in his hole! "That's my hole!" said Jimmy.

"I am a little bird sitting on a nest," said Janet.

"That is not a nest!" yelled Jimmy.
"That is my hole, and I want to dig in it!"

"Children!" said the twins' mother. "Janet, let Jimmy have his hole. It's his, because he dug it."

"I just wanted to borrow Jimmy's hole for a little while," said Janet, as she climbed out and went to play on the slide.

"I don't want Janet to borrow my hole," said
Jimmy, and he began to dig with his real shovel.
He dug and dug. Push, lift, toss. The hole grew
deeper and deeper. Pretty soon it was up to
Jimmy's knees. Still Jimmy dug. He had never
worked so hard, but of course he had never had a
real shovel to work with before. Then some dirt
around the edge of the hole fell into the hole
and buried Jimmy's shoes. Jimmy was not
discouraged.

He pulled his feet out of the dirt, shoveled the dirt out of the hole, and went on digging. "Jimmy, you look so hot and tired," said his mother. "Why don't you rest awhile?"

"No," said Jimmy. "I'm digging the biggest hole in the world." Pretty soon Jimmy's mother and father came to look at the hole.

"My goodness," said his mother. "What are you going to do with such a great big hole?"

"We could pretend it is a place to catch fish," said Janet. "I could tie a string to a stick and pretend I am catching fish."

"No," said Jimmy. "It isn't a place to catch fish. It is a real big hole."

"What are you going to do with your real hole?" asked his father.

"We could pretend it is a place where baby rabbits live," said Janet. "I could get in the hole and pretend I am a baby rabbit."

"No!" said Jimmy. "It isn't a place where baby rabbits live. It is a real hole, and I made it with a real shovel."

Then the lady who lived next door came over to see Jimmy's hole. "My, what a big hole!" she said. "What are you going to do with such a great big hole?" Jimmy did not know what he was going to do with such a great big hole. Muffy, the dog who lived next door, came over and sniffed the hole.

"Muffy could bury bones in the hole," said Janet.

"No!" said Jimmy. "Muffy can dig his own hole."

Then the man who lived next door came to see Jimmy's hole. "Say, that is a big hole!" he said. "What are you going to do with such a big hole?" Everybody thought Jimmy should do something with his hole. Everybody but Jimmy. He liked his hole just the way it was.

"I am going to keep my hole," he said.

"I'm afraid not," said his father. "If you or Janet ran across the yard and fell into the hole, you might get hurt." Jimmy looked at his father. Not keep his real hole that he had dug with his real shovel?

"I want to keep my hole," he said.

"Now Jimmy," said his father. "I don't want you or Janet to get hurt."

"You said I could dig a big hole," Jimmy reminded him.

"Yes, but I didn't know you could dig such a big hole," answered his father. This made Jimmy feel better. His father hadn't known he could dig such a big hole.

"There must be something we could do with such a nice hole," said Jimmy's mother. "It's too bad not to use it for something, when Jimmy has worked so hard." So Jimmy and Janet and their mother and father thought and thought. What could they do with such a big hole?

"I know!" said Jimmy's father.

"What?" asked Jimmy and Janet. "You wait and see. It's a surprise," answered their father, and he backed the car out of the garage and drove away.

"What do you suppose he's going to get?" asked the twins' mother.

"Is it a big water pipe?" asked Jimmy.

"Is it a family of baby rabbits?" asked Janet.

"I don't know," answered their mother. "We will have to wait and see."

After a while Jimmy and Janet's father came back. When he got out of the car he took something out of the backseat. It was a tree growing in a big tin can. "Is it a real tree?" asked Jimmy.

"Yes, it's a real spruce tree," answered his father, "and your hole is just the right size to plant it in." Jimmy grabbed his shovel. He wanted to help plant a real tree in his real hole.

His father took the tree out
of the can and set it in the hole.

With the hose they watered
the roots of the tree.

Then they filled in the hole with dirt.

"Now we have a real tree growing in our yard,"
said Jimmy's mother.

"We can pretend it's a Christmas tree," said Janet.

"It is a Christmas tree," said her father. "This year
we can have two Christmas trees, one in the house
and one in the yard."

"You didn't know I could dig a hole for a tree,"
said Jimmy, who was pleased with what he had done.
"No, we didn't," said Jimmy's mother. Then she
brushed the dirt off Jimmy's jeans and emptied the
dirt out of Jimmy's shoes.

"It was a real grown-up hole," Jimmy said proudly.

"Yes, sir!" said Jimmy's father. "A real grown-up hole!"